No Scythes in the Tea Tent

&

Other Stories

Hazel Leventhal

TSL Publications

First published in Great Britain in 2025
By TSL Publications, Rickmansworth

ISBN: 978-1-917426-30-5

Cover image courtesy of
Larry Leventhal

Contents

For my

grandchildren,

Jack, Lucy and Bea.

1. No Scythes in the Tea Tent

It was the weekend of the Green Scythe Fair and Daddy was going to be teaching scything. He was also going to help out in the tea tent during the afternoon and said that I could help him. Mummy took me to the fair but she didn't stay for long. They never stay around each other much. Sometimes if I'm staying with Daddy and he drops me home I ask him to stay for dinner and he always says, "If Mummy doesn't mind." She usually nods and then he stays but eats quickly and goes as soon as he finishes. When we're at his house he's much slower and spends time talking to me. I asked him once about this and he said that he and Mummy used to love each other but then Mummy said she didn't love him anymore so that's why they don't live together any longer. He had to leave. At first he had to sleep in his car as he had nowhere to go but then he sold his flat in London, which he had been renting out, so he was able to buy his little house.

I see Daddy about twice a week, sometimes more, but when we're together we do everything with each other and he always makes things such fun. He takes me swimming in the summer and to soft play in the winter and we spend a lot of time in his garden where he grows lots of things. I like to help him by watering with the watering can and I love picking the strawberries and raspberries and goose-berries. He grows lots of other things as well like potatoes and onions but they're not that interesting and I can't pick them and eat them straight from the ground. He likes cooking them though. He cooks me dinner when I'm with him and we also have a lot of hummus with strips of red and yellow peppers. I especially like pickled cucumbers. They're my favourite.

Daddy has told me many times that scythes are very dangerous and I mustn't touch them. He keeps his one very sharp by doing something he calls peening, which means sharpening the blade. Scythes are very long and the blades are shiny and can cut through lots of tall grass. He scythes big fields and orchards for people and sometimes does smaller lawns in gardens. He also does gardening for people but always plays with me on the days I see him. He makes up lovely games like the one we play in the park where he tucks my skipping rope into the back of his trousers so it's like a tail and I have to try and catch it. It's great fun and we do a lot of running round the park. Sometimes he ties the skipping rope round my waist and he chases me and I always finish up laughing so much I fall over. He also plays tea parties with my toys but I'm getting a bit old for that now. I'll be five next birthday and have just started school so I like to play schools instead.

Last week I was a little fox all week and he made a big obstacle course downstairs for me to run through with places for me to hide in or climb over. It was a good obstacle course. We also do painting together. He has a conservatory where we both put up our easels and he ties a big apron round me and we paint, which is something I really like to do. I think I want to be a painter when I grow up. Mummy lets me paint as well but she doesn't join in. She usually reads a book while I'm painting or sometimes does some cooking or something else.

When I'm with Daddy we sometimes visit a friend of his who has a dog and I like to play with her too. He said he might get a dog one day but that dogs are expensive and he can't afford one at the moment.

There are lots of things he can't afford but he doesn't seem to mind. He said people rely too much on things and we should all try to live more sustainably. I'm not really sure what that means but it seems to be important.

There's a pond in Daddy's garden with water lilies and tadpoles and sometimes a few little fish. I like to dabble my hands in the water and watch the little creatures scurrying around in the water. There's also a slide and a swing which he put in the garden just for me. They're bright yellow and blue and I like to play on them. At the back of the garden there's a big field which looks like it goes on for miles. When I'm in the garden I like to look for wood lice which I pick up and look after for a while.

I get lots of clothes from my cousin, Daddy's brother's little girl. Her name is Lucy and she is five years older than me. She has a brother two years older than her. Sometimes we have video calls with them and last summer they came down for a holiday so we could all be together. They stayed in a big house with a swimming pool and we visited them a few days during the week they were here. That was great fun and Lucy used to give me piggy back rides and they both played with me. I think they're coming again this summer so that's something to look forward to. Nanny and Poppa are coming too. They're Daddy's Mummy and Daddy. Mummy's Mum is called Grandma and her husband is called Gramps. He isn't Mummy's Daddy, just what's called a step-daddy. Nobody in my family has a Daddy living with them. Nanny and Poppa live a long way away and I don't remember visiting them but Daddy said I did go with him and Mummy when I was a baby. They come to see us when they can and usually near my birthday and always bring me birthday presents.

The Green Scythe Fair takes place over a whole weekend and lots of people come to it. They have tents for different things and people sell things they've made as well as the people learning how to scythe. There's a tea tent and Daddy is helping out making tea for people during the afternoon. He said I can help but mustn't touch the big kettle as it's very hot and much too big for me to pick up. I can help with the water though and when people come in and just want a glass of water I can pour it from one of two jugs. They're quite big too but I can lift them and pour out the water and I do it very carefully. I try not to spill a drop.

Sometimes Mummy's sister comes with

her little girl, Lily. Lily is the same age as Lucy and she also goes to stay with her Daddy but mainly lives with her Mummy. Mummy and her sisters don't seem to like living with men, only women and their children. When I grow up I think I might like to live with the Daddy as well. I don't know why they don't seem to like daddies. I think Daddy is more fun than Mummy who doesn't usually play with me. She never does anything she doesn't want to do so if I want to do something and she says, "No, I don't want to do that" then I just have to do it on my own.

Daddy said he was very pleased with the way I was helping with the water and I also give people biscuits if they want them. I put the biscuits out on a plate and people help themselves when they have a cup of tea. One man walked into the tent carrying his scythe. He walked over towards the tea kettle but I called out to him in as loud a voice as I could: "No scythes in the tea tent please."

2. Flight to Budapest

It was the middle of August and John had to go to a conference in Budapest. It was for four days and he suggested I fly out to join him on the Thursday and we could spend the weekend together. I'd never been to Budapest and was looking forward to it. My flight from Heathrow was in the afternoon and was due to land in Budapest at around 6 p.m. It wasn't that full and I sat in a window seat and a young Japanese man was sitting in the aisle seat and no one between us. I had written the telephone number of John's hotel on my ticket just in case.

The flight left on time and I was reading *The Making and Breaking of Affectional Bonds* by John Bowlby and found it absorbing. As we flew I noticed the sky was getting darker and about half-way through the flight we hit a terrible storm, a real humdinger: great flashes of lightning, huge claps of thunder and torrential rain. The plane was buffeted about like a little cork on a stormy sea. They announced that we all had to put our seatbelts on but nothing else was said.

The plane was jouncing around and it was only the seatbelts keeping us in place. I went on with my book but noticed the Japanese man had adopted the brace position (not that anyone had told us to) and he was clearly terrified. I put my book down and said, "Don't worry. It'll be all right."

He looked at me rather crossly and said, "How you know?"

I just said I knew and asked him how old he was.

"Twenty-one," he replied. He was just between the ages of our own two sons of 22 and 20. I asked him why he was going to Budapest and he said it was to do with work and he had an important meeting there in the morning. I said I was meeting my husband who was at a conference.

The plane continued to shudder and judder, up and down, bobbing like a cork and people were getting restless. This lasted for well over an hour and no one was telling us anything. There were some children crying and mothers trying to hush them. I continued to read my book. Eventually it was announced that due to the extreme weather conditions our pilot couldn't land in Budapest so we were re-routing to the nearest airport which was

Brno in the Czech Republic. We continued flying for another two hours or so. At last it was announced that we would be landing, which we did, and lots of people cheered. As we unfastened our seatbelts the Japanese man asked me, "How could you go on weeding?" I just smiled and said it seemed the best thing to do. Most people then started making phone calls on their mobiles but at that time I didn't have a mobile. After he'd made a call the Japanese man asked if I would like to make a call. I thanked him and showed him the hotel's number on my ticket. He dialled it for me and handed me his phone. When it was answered I asked to speak to John and they put me through to his room. There was no answer. I left a message saying that due to the storm we'd been diverted to Brno and that somehow I supposed we'd get back to Budapest airport.

We were then all shepherded off the plane and into the tiny airport. One of the air stewardesses said that coaches would come to take us back to Budapest airport but they might take some time. We all sat in the small lounge and young Japanese man attached himself to me. There was another middle-aged businessman who also seemed to be alone who attached himself to us. There was no food or drink available as it was too late for any of the shops to be open. There was a slot machine which sold crisps, chocolate and drinks. We waited. It was about 10 p.m.

After a couple of hours they told us that the first coach was arriving and that they would need about three coaches to transport all of us so in the first coach it would be women and children only. I waited in turn to board the coach and when all the women and children were on board it was seen there were two spare seats so young Japanese man and middle-aged businessman joined me. We then began the drive to Budapest. I thought that at that time of night the roads would be fairly clear but not at all. It was like a non-stop traffic jam all the way. We eventually arrived at Budapest airport at about 5.30 a.m. I had tried to snooze a bit on the coach but hadn't really had much sleep so felt a bit light-headed.

Once we were back at the airport we all left the coach and there was a scramble for taxis. Japanese man, businessman and I shared a taxi and we drove into the centre of Budapest. We dropped off the businessman at his hotel first and then it was my hotel. I said goodbye to the young Japanese man and he shook my hand and thanked me for keeping him calm. It was now about 6 a.m. I trundled my little case into the hotel and approached the reception where one man was sitting reading a paper. I explained who I was and that I would like to join my husband in his room. He looked at me suspiciously and asked to see my passport, which I duly showed him. He studied it carefully then handed me a door key and said to go up to the third floor. I went up to the third floor, opened the door very quietly and went into the room. John immediately sat up in bed, looked at me and said, "You're late." That was his sense of humour. "I know," I said. "I'm exhausted. I'm just going to have a quick wash then I must have a rest. Wake me up about 9ish as I don't want to miss any of our sightseeing." I lay down next to him and promptly fell asleep. Later that morning we started to explore Budapest, although I was feeling somewhat spaced out.

3. Meeting For Lunch

We'd been meeting for lunch for nearly 40 years. I first met Remy when she came to work as a temp at the firm where I worked. I was the PA/Secretary to the senior partner and to the team of architects who worked for him. Remy worked for one of the other teams but often popped into my office for a chat. My days were busy. When I arrived I would go up to the third floor and wait for a call from my boss, which usually came at 9 a.m. prompt. I would go down to his office on the ground floor and he would dictate letters for most of the morning. We would go through his post together and I would separate them into little piles for the various project architects. He would do letters to the firm's solicitors and accountants as well as the usual ones to structural engineers, planning officers, site managers and various heads of the companies we worked with. After he'd finished I would take the letters round to the different project architects and then go back up to the third floor and start typing the correspondence. Throughout the day different architects would come upstairs and leave hand-written letters or site meeting minutes or accounts for me to type in the basket on my desk. When I'd finished my boss's letters, which could take well into the afternoon, I would start the rest that were in the basket. During this time I would take telephone calls and book train tickets and arrange the various lunches my boss was organising.

Every month he had a Connaught lunch, which was a lunch for business colleagues at The Connaught Hotel, and I would speak to the chef on a regular basis. I remember once a secretary of one of his guests rang me to explain that her boss had an ulcer and had to be careful with what he ate. We went through what he could and couldn't have and I then rang the chef at The Connaught and told him. He suggested that he should have a chicken dish with rice and I said that sounded fine and asked about dessert, as the desserts on offer seemed too rich for him. He said "How about rice pudding?" I commented that he was already having rice with his main course and I could hear the chef drawing himself up and then he said, enunciating every work extremely clearly, "Madam, we are *renowned* for our rice pudding." I couldn't argue.

I shared my office with the secretary to the Office Manager and people were often popping in and out so it was a sociable and busy little hub of activity. Remy had trained as a teacher but decided at some point that the pay wasn't good enough so decided to do secretarial work instead. She was small, just about 5', with large dark eyes and black hair in an elfin cut which actually suited her. She was a few years older than me but still lived with her parents. She was amusing and I found her refreshing and we sometimes went out for lunch together. We found we shared a liking for books and films and so started to go to the cinema or theatre some evenings and would talk about the latest books we'd read. Our friendship developed. She didn't stay with the firm for long, maybe four or five months, but by the time she left we'd established a good rapport and so decided we'd meet up regularly and keep in touch.

For the first few years we met regularly for lunch dates and also some-times in the evenings. I remember we went to see the Eric Rohmer film, 'Claire's Knee', which we both enjoyed. We also went to the theatre a couple of times. Remy was in a relationship at the time and had been living with her boyfriend. One evening she rang me in rather an agitated state. She told me that she'd become pregnant but knew she couldn't have the baby and so had arranged to have an abortion. She didn't want her parents to know and wondered if I could collect her from the hospital after the abortion as they didn't want her to be on her own the first night. She asked if she could come and stay with me that night. I felt saddened by her news, particularly as I felt she could have had the baby but knew that wasn't my business. I agreed to collect her from the hospital and let her stay overnight with me. She looked white and exhausted when I collected her and we didn't talk about it as she said she didn't want to discuss it at all. My parents knew nothing about it and just thought she was coming to stay overnight with me after going out together. Remy had been sharing a flat with the father of her now aborted baby and continued to live there.

Soon after that I became engaged and Remy did me the great honour of accepting an invitation to our wedding as normally she hated such formal events and wouldn't attend them, even ones in her own family. We continued to see each other for lunches over the coming months and years. Her father died and so she went back to live with her mother but she had cannily bought some more property of her own, which she managed and rented out so she made a good income as a landlady. She took her responsibilities seriously and was always going round to fix things in the two flats she'd bought and make them better for her tenants. She'd also changed her job again and after a while as a secretary to one of the professors at Birkbeck College she went back into teaching.

The years went on. I had two children and during the summer holidays I sometimes met up with Remy with my sons. I remember one occasion where we took a riverboat down the Thames to Greenwich and another time we met up in Regent's Park. She thought my sons were very naughty even though they behaved like most other young boys. I used to think that maybe some of her pupils were frightened of her. She taught primary age children and I did wonder if some of them used to dread going to school because of her.

We would meet for lunch every few weeks and I became used to the pattern of our meetings. One of us would arrive at the restaurant we'd chosen and if I was first I'd sit at a table and wait for Remy. As soon as she arrived she would want to change the table we were sitting at. I don't recall us ever sitting at the table I'd chosen. I often had to wait for her as she was invariably late. When we'd ordered our food she would often complain about the meal or ask for something different as she hadn't realised it contained some ingredient she didn't want. She used to smother her food with copious amounts of salt and pepper. She was still amusing and told funny stories about the people she worked with and we discussed world events as well as the most recent books and films we'd seen.

In between our meetings we would usually speak on the phone fairly regularly as well. Remy had an older brother, with whom she had a prickly relationship. After her father died and she had gone back to live with her mother, she found herself having many arguments with her brother as to how to look after their mother. She employed carers to come in and help her mother while she was at work and she took it upon herself to become her mother's carer. One day her brother visited and during an argument he slammed her head against a wall and behaved in a very threatening manner. She was furious and sought legal advice about obtaining an injunction to stop him coming near her. This was something she spoke about at length for many months.

Her mother was getting frail as she aged and Remy took great pains to provide her with the best possible care but one day while Remy was at work her mother tripped and fell. She had to go into hospital and died shortly afterwards. Remy was inconsolable. While her mother was in hospital her brother came to visit her at the hospital. He was nervous to come in to see her due to the injunction so Remy went into the corridor and said of course he could visit their mother. Afterwards they had a coffee together in the hospital canteen. This mended the rupture between them. Afterwards Remy was so grief-stricken and for some reason felt guilty about her mother's death. For about nine months I became her unofficial counsellor as every conversation we had centred around her grief and the loss of her mother. We spent many hours talking things through and I tried to reassure her that she had done everything possible to look after her mother as best she could. The pain she felt was understandable and grief is the price we all pay for love.

During this time Remy joined a gym as

a way of working through her grief. She developed a love of running and would tell me in great detail about her gym sessions and how much she enjoyed running on the treadmill and doing spin classes. She began to go to the gym every day. She also became obsessed about what she ate and planned her meals carefully. She told me once that she made herself egg-white omelettes. I asked what she did with the egg yolks and she said, "I throw them away." This rather horrified me but I didn't like to say anything.

Remy also spent many hours and a lot of money on beauty treatments and at one of our lunches told me she was going into hospital the following week to have an operation to "improve" her eyes. I was a bit dubious but if it made her happy then I wasn't going to argue. One didn't argue with Remy anyway because it wasn't worth the energy. She was always right and always vociferous in her opinions. Over the years I had noticed that she didn't seem to have much of a sense of humour. I was sure she used to laugh at things I told her but not any longer. Sometimes I told her little jokes I'd heard but she always maintained a stony silence, never once laughing at any of them. I stopped telling them. She told me once that she didn't like Charlie Chaplin and couldn't see why people found him funny. I felt that said it all.

Over the years we met less frequently as we both had busy lives and since her mother died she became more and more involved with her gym sessions and maintaining the various properties she owned and let out. She did agree to come to our son's wedding though, again a great honour. I'm not sure she particularly enjoyed it as she sat grim-faced during the best man's speech, which everyone else found hilariously funny but she clearly did not.

A few months later we were talking on the phone and I said that my daughter-in-law had gone for her first scan as she was now pregnant. She interrupted me and said, "I don't want to talk about babies." It flashed through my mind the innumerable hours I had spent listening to her talking about her brother, the grief about her mother, her gym sessions and many other topics. I was stunned at her comment. I put the phone down. That was the end of our meetings for lunch.

4. A Walk At Dusk

It was a warm summer's evening and I was feeling restless. Jenny was reading quietly and didn't want to be disturbed. Our parents were on holiday, a Mediterranean cruise, so Jenny and I had the flat to ourselves. We always got on well together but this evening I was feeling a bit claustrophobic and needed to get out for a while. I decided to visit my friend Helen who lived about a half hour's walk away. I told Jenny I'd be going there but would definitely be home by 10.30. It was late June so stayed light until then. Jenny nodded and seemed happy for me to leave her on her own.

I brushed my hair and set off. There was no need to ring Helen first. We often used to pop in to see each other. I knew it would be fine. It was such a lovely evening. I had been walking for about 15 minutes and had reached the dual carriageway which led up to Helen's house. I noticed a car on the other side of the road which kept stopping a little way ahead of me, waiting until I walked past it and then carrying on but then stopping again a little further ahead.

It didn't bother me too much as it was the other side of the dual carriageway. As I continued walking I realised I was coming to some allotments on my right and there were no more houses until Helen's turning. I looked to see if the car was still ahead but it seemed to have gone so I continued walking.

After another few minutes I saw the same car driving down towards me on my side of the road now. This made me feel somewhat anxious. It pulled up and waited for me to come close and the driver, a large dark-haired man, leaned over towards the passenger side and wound down the window. It looked as though he was going to ask for directions but I didn't like the look of him and just walked past. He drove off.

A few minutes later I saw him on the other side of the road again and realised he'd gone to the roundabout and turned round. He was now on the opposite side of the road again but I felt he was probably going to the next roundabout and coming back down on the same side I was on. I decided to turn round and walk back to where there were houses. As I walked towards the first turning on my left the car approached again. It overtook me and stopped. My heart stopped. The driver opened his door and got out. I felt quite panicked by now and began to run. He got back in his car and followed me. I turned left and he followed and overtook me. I didn't know what to do as he was beginning to get out of the car again. I noticed a door to one of the houses was open. I ran towards it and ran inside. There was a small hallway and an open door into a living room. Inside was a family with three children. They stared at me in astonishment and I stood there gasping for breath. The mother got up and asked me what was wrong. When I'd got my breath back I explained about being followed by the man in the car and how frightening it was. Her husband looked outside but the car had gone. He said he'd ring the police and did so. I spoke to someone and again explained what had happened but, of course, I hadn't noted the car's number and couldn't give much of a description of the man or the car. The policeman said there wasn't much they could do.

The woman kindly offered to give me a lift home so I accepted and apologised for having given them all a fright. She was very kind and understanding and said it was perfectly all right. She then drove me home again. When I opened our front door Jenny looked up and remarked that I hadn't been gone that long. I told her what had happened. She could see I was still shaken and we decided that all's well that ends well and we wouldn't say anything about this incident when our parents came home.

A week later they came home and we spent their first evening chatting with them telling us all about their lovely holiday. My father decided he was tired and went to bed. As soon as he was gone my mother turned to me and said, "What were you doing last Wednesday evening between about 8 and 9?"

I went a bit cold and said, "Why do you ask?"

"Well," she said, "I was up on deck after dinner and I suddenly knew that you were in the most terrible danger. I was really worried for you. I stood there looking out to sea and I prayed very hard for about 20 minutes and then suddenly I knew the danger was over. So, what was happening?" I told her about what had happened and Jenny and I looked at each other. How could my mother have known I was in danger? Was this a mother's intuition or what?

5. Imaginary Friends

He always was other-worldly. I remember one morning when Claire popped in for a coffee after dropping her girls at school. Jacob hadn't woken up yet so I wasn't disturbing him. After she'd had her coffee I said I'd better go upstairs to see if he was awake yet.

"Doesn't he cry for you when he wakes up?" she asked.

"Not always," I said. "Sometimes he just lies in his cot quietly."

We went upstairs and into Jacob's room. He was lying in his cot and turned his head towards us. He stared at us both with his big, dark eyes and Claire said, "Ooh, he's been here before, hasn't he?"

One morning I was cooking in the kitchen and Jacob was playing on the floor in the living room. He was about eight months old and hadn't learnt to crawl yet. His older brother had learned to crawl at six months and used to scoot around our flat like a little dynamo getting into every nook and cranny so we had to cover up all electricity points and anything else that might be dangerous. Jacob was content to sit and point at things for his brother to bring to him. This particular morning I'd put out a few toys for him to play with and the door between the kitchen and living room was open so I could hear him. Suddenly, for no explicable reason, I rushed into the living room to find Jacob scarlet in the face with the cord from his Fisher-Price telephone wrapped around his neck. It had been a hand-me-down toy from one of his cousins and I believe Fisher-Price shortened the cord later on. He'd somehow become entangled and was strangling himself. I quickly extricated him and soothed his terrified crying afterwards. I brought him into the kitchen and sat him in his highchair to play safely within view after that. Sometimes he used to babble as though talking to someone but I thought nothing of it.

When he was about four he had two imaginary friends, Clink and Tink. He used to play with them all the time. I would often hear him talking to them and laughing. He was quite open about their friendship and it didn't interfere with anything so I was quite happy for him to have imaginary friends and didn't worry about it or wonder who they were.

One morning we'd dropped Adam off at school and were out shopping. Jacob went to afternoon nursery so we spent the mornings together and I took him after lunch for his afternoon session. He enjoyed nursery school and looked forward to it. We bought some fish at the fish van for lunch. Jacob was wearing his Spiderman costume and was jumping around, striking poses, totally immersed in being Spiderman. I said we needed to get home quite quickly as I had to unpack the shopping and make lunch and he would have to change into something else for nursery.

As we were driving up Evelyn Drive he said to me, rather sadly, "Mummy, Clink and Tink won't be coming to play with me anymore."

"Oh," I said. "Why not?"

"Well, they're really dead children and they told me they're going to play with someone else now."

I nearly crashed the car.

6. You're Not Going Anywhere

It was the third time I'd been sent to hospital. It was mid-2020, Covid was rampant, hospitals were full and people avoided them if possible. My GP had sent me for a blood test as my last two had been so deranged and I'd been sent into hospital for various transfusions. It had all started after some infection or bug or virus in April 2020 just at the start of the pandemic. Normally I would have been investigated in hospital but under the circumstances of that time I was just left until my GP decided to do blood tests to check on how I was. Not good was the answer.

Even though I'd been sent at the request of my GP I still had to wait for hours in A&E. Eventually I was sent to a ward and put into a side room. After another couple of hours a young doctor came in and closed the door behind him. He sat down on the chair beside my trolley and looked at my blood test results. "Well," he said, "however much we put the foot on the pedal, you're not going anywhere."

I was stunned into momentary silence and then said, "So, what do you suggest happens?"

He sighed wearily. "I suppose we can give you a blood transfusion and then you can come back every few weeks for another one."

At that he left the room and I sat trying to comprehend what had just happened. After a few moments a wave of anger washed over me and I got up and walked out to the nurses' station and asked if I could call my husband. I sat there while nurses and other staff bustled around me and spoke to Barry. I told him exactly what the doctor had said and he felt as angry as I did. He said he'd speak to our GP and I went back to the little room. After a while one of the nurses came in and told me my husband had called back and spoken to the doctor who had seen me. They'd had "a bit of a contretemps" according to the nurse and then the young doctor reappeared and said, "Your husband has been on the line and has told me that he won't come to collect you until we've come up with a treatment plan." He looked at me rather crossly and walked out again. After waiting in there for another hour or so I was transferred to a ward.

I was put in the first bed in the 8-bedded ward. Next to me was an extremely large young woman who seemed to be most uncomfortable. She was sitting upright on the side of the bed and had an oxygen mask on. She smiled at me and said she couldn't lie down as it was too uncomfortable and that she was suffering from water retention. She certainly looked waterlogged and I reckoned she must weigh about 25 stone. I asked how long she'd been in hospital and she said she'd been there for three weeks. Opposite me was an old lady who was under the covers and was as thin as the woman next to me was fat. She barely made an impression under the blankets. She seemed to be asleep. One of the nurses came in and began taking everyone's blood pressure and temperatures. I lay back and wondered how long I would be there and what they would do.

The evening meal arrived and I was given a tray with the meal the previous occupant had ordered. Unfortunately, as I'm coeliac, I couldn't eat it. I explained this to the nurse and she whisked it away and said she'd try and find me something. A bit later on she came in again and with a red marker pen wrote "gluten-free" on the board above my bed. I was relieved she'd done that as it saved me explaining each time. After another few minutes she returned with a tray with a sealed meal on it which turned out to be one of the gluten-free options available. There were about five options and I soon became familiar with all of them, two of which were edible.

It was night-time and the lights were dimmed. I was opposite a door that opened onto a stores cupboard and every time a member of staff came in to get something out of that cupboard as soon as the door was opened bright fluorescent lighting flooded the room. This happened dozens of times during the night with the consequence that I had hardly any sleep. The constant burst of brightness didn't matter too much though because the woman in the bed opposite was now wakeful. Quiet as she'd been during the day, the night seemed to energise her and she didn't stop talking and muttering to herself and then saying over and over, "Billeee, Billee, don't leave me Billee. I love you Billee. Come back to me Billee." This was repeated over and over again and it took every reserve of patience not to say anything back to her.

In the morning the lights were put on again and the morning routines began. Breakfast was brought in and a nurse sat by the old lady's bed trying to get her to eat something. Further down the ward was another old lady who was refusing all food and would only drink some tea and eat some ice cream at lunch time. I think she was living off tea and ice cream which was not really enough to sustain her. She couldn't get out of bed and she could no longer walk. She was unnervingly thin.

The other beds had other women suffering from various chronic conditions and doctors and nurses came and went, drawing the blue curtains around the beds while they examined their patients or carried out procedures. Soon a posse of doctors arrived. The morning ward round. They stopped at my bed and one of them looked at my notes and then looked at me. He asked me how I was feeling and I said I felt very weak and tired. He nodded and said I was severely anaemic and would need a blood transfusion. He then looked more closely at my blood test results. "Has anyone suggested you have EPO injections?" he asked. "No," I said. "I've never heard of them. What are they?" "They're injections of a substance that most people make naturally and your kidneys make haemoglobin but yours don't as your kidney function is very low. You're probably going to need dialysis but EPO injections would stimulate your kidneys to make more haemoglobin which would help with your anaemia. It will take some time but will definitely help." I thanked him and asked if I could start these injections soon and he said he'd organise it. In the meantime I'd have a blood transfusion and would probably be discharged.

That evening things were set up for me to have the blood transfusion. I was told it would take about an hour. In the event it took two and a half hours. By the time it was finished all the lights were out and most people were sleeping apart from the lady in the bed opposite who had started calling out to Billy once again. She continued, on and off, throughout the night. Also a new patient arrived so there was quite a bit of disturbance as she was wheeled in and put to bed and doctors came to examine her.

In the morning I did feel stronger, having had a litre of blood infused, and was hopeful that I would be sent home. The morning routines took place and a phlebotomist came to take my blood, always a difficult task as my puny veins refused to co-operate. As they'd done what they could they discharged me. Once home I still felt weak and permanently exhausted. More worryingly, I kept falling over and sometimes fainting. As I'm 5'8" tall it was difficult to help me up again but somehow we managed it but it was a struggle. My doctor sent me for more blood tests. The results were not good.

As I was still anaemic and so low in many vital nutrients I was sent back to hospital and again had to wait hours in A&E despite them knowing exactly why I'd been sent in. This time they decided to feed me intravenously. Soon I was back in my old bed and hooked up to a machine that delivered liquid nourishment continuously. I lay watching the comings and goings of the ward. The large lady next to me had been moved to another ward and an older woman took her place. She was brought in while the other woman was still there and sat waiting by the side of the bed. Once she was installed in the bed she commented on the size of the previous occupant. I told her that she was suffering from water retention. She snorted and said "Water retention! That's not water retention. That's gluttony." I kept quiet.

As it was the time of Covid there were no visitors allowed and the days were long and boring. There was nothing to alleviate the boredom as they didn't have television or radio or anything to distract one from the tedium of hospital life. They still brought meals but the choices for me were limited and I didn't feel like eating anyway. As I was marooned like a beached whale with tubes going into each arm and a nasal gastric tube as well I was more or less immobile. I felt cold all the time and the nurses would tuck blankets round me so I was like a cocoon on the bed.

Each morning the phlebotomists came round to take blood but they always had a struggle with my veins. After a couple of weeks of this when they would leave me as they couldn't get at my blood, they took me down to the operating theatre to have a PICC line inserted into my left arm. This was to enable them to access my blood more easily. This vital information didn't seem to be passed on to other medical staff so each morning began with a phlebotomist trying to get my blood in the usual manner and each morning I had to tell them I had a PICC line to make this procedure easier. I don't know why staff are not told these things but it happened in all areas. The left hand never knew what the right hand was doing and this was true in every aspect of hospital life. I think that's why so many things become a problem. There is virtually no communication between departments and certainly none between doctors and nurses.

Further down the ward doctors were round the bed of the woman who was refusing to eat, apart from ice cream. The doctor sat on the side of her bed and said, "If you don't eat something then you are going to die." She said, "I know." The doctors moved on to the next patient. I wondered why she was refusing to eat and wondered why they hadn't asked her this simple question or if there was some food that she might try.

They were still bringing me food as well as the intravenous nourishment and I picked at it as best I could. The weekly weigh-ins showed I was steadily losing weight. One morning another young doctor came on a ward round and asked me in an exasperated tone, "Why don't you just eat?" I was silent for a moment and then said wearily: "I have coeliac disease and chronic kidney disease and it's difficult to find food that's compatible with both those restrictions in here ... plus, I had a severe bout of vomiting and diarrhoea in April and some things still make me throw up. Given those three factors I don't think it's unreasonable that I have a certain reluctance to eat." He pursed his lips and turned away.

One morning I woke up unable to see properly out of my right eye so I mentioned this to one of the doctors when they came round. They had a short discussion and then said I was probably suffering from a Vitamin A deficiency and left it at that. I accepted this explanation and didn't think to question it and hoped that the feeding would address this deficiency.

After a few weeks, by which time I think they felt they'd "fattened me up" enough, they took me off the intravenous feeding. What a relief that was. When they finally took the naso-gastric tube out I felt jubilant. Unfortunately, as I'd been bedbound for so long, I could barely walk. They sent the physiotherapists to prepare me for discharge. Each day they came and managed to haul me out of bed and into a chair. It took supreme effort for me to get up out of that chair and I struggled with it for some time. Luckily one of the physiotherapists was a tall, well-built woman who was able to help me. She pulled as I pushed and between us I managed to get on my feet. Once on my feet, with the aid of a walker, I could walk about reasonably well. I practised diligently and trundled down to the end of the ward to look out of the window. I hadn't been outside for over six weeks and hadn't looked out of a window during that time either. I'd seen the window from my bed but could only see some of the sky while lying down. At the end of the ward the very thin lady who refused to eat was lying in her bed. She was so thin that it was painful to look at her. I stopped at the end of her bed and said, "Hello."

She smiled and said, "Hello, it's good to see you up and about."

I asked how long she'd been there and she said, "About two months." She said she didn't really want to go home as her husband didn't want to look after her and she had two sons who wouldn't be any help so she preferred to stay in bed in hospital. I asked if she used to work and she said, "Yes, I was a nanny." This came as a surprise and she said she used to love her work and kept in touch with many of the children she'd looked after. She gave it up when she had her own two children and said that life was never the same again. I asked her why she didn't eat anything and she said she didn't like any of the food except for the ice cream and she didn't feel hungry anyway. She said she probably wouldn't be able to stand now even though they kept trying to get her out of bed. Her legs certainly didn't look strong enough to support her. She said she liked looking out of the window and didn't care that she would never be going home again.

I walked back to my own bed stopping to chat to one or two of the others on my way. Most of them said they were pleased to see me up and about. Later that day one of the doctors informed me that as my kidney function was only 8% I would need to start dialysis but before that could happen they'd have to do a small operation to create a fistula in my arm to create a good access point to allow for the tube. We were approaching the third lockdown in November 2020 and they wanted to discharge as many patients as possible before then.

I was discharged on 5th November and came home with a panoply of aids such as a walker and a huge supply of nutritional drinks. The first week at home they sent in carers in the morning to help me shower and dress. I didn't like having these carers coming in each morning, especially when some of them were men, and was glad when the first week was over. During the day I practised walking down the corridor between my bedroom and the living room and after about three weeks I was able to do it without the aid of the walker.

Mealtimes became a bit of a problem as my husband can't cook and wasn't interested in learning to cook so we were relying heavily on ready meals but they had to be gluten-free so it was all a bit of a challenge. I did go into the kitchen and made a few simple meals but my energy levels were so low that standing for more than a few minutes was exhausting. Afterwards I would have to go and lie down and usually fell asleep for half an hour or so. I had to have frequent naps during the day and went to bed early.

My strength gradually improved a bit and one day I said that I really needed to get my eyes checked as I still couldn't see well out of my right eye. Once lockdown was over we arranged to see an optician. After the eye examination she informed me that I needed to see an ophthalmologist as there was something behind my right eye that needed investigating. We decided to go privately initially as this would be covered by our health insurance. The ophthalmologist did various tests and scans and told me I had suffered a central retinol vein occlusion or, to put it in layman's language, a stroke behind the eye. This would necessitate me having injections into my eye to clear the build-up of blood that had accumulated. I didn't like the sound of it as most people are squeamish about eyes and I was no exception. The first injection was arranged and I was fairly nervous beforehand but he was very gentle and the anaesthetic meant I didn't feel anything. The next morning my eye was terribly bloodshot and I looked like someone out of a horror film but it cleared within the next few days. Since then I have had to have regular injections every eight weeks or so and one gets used to anything. Thankfully this has kept the sight in my right eye although it is as though I am looking underwater in that eye, kind of wavy and distorted. That's one of the reasons I decided to give up driving. I felt it would be irresponsible to continue particularly as my energy levels are low and sometimes just "go" as though I've hit a brick wall. That wouldn't be clever if I was driving and knew that I just had to stop or collapse.

A few months after leaving hospital I was called in again to have an operation to create the fistula in my right arm. It was done under local anaesthetic so I was awake and chatting to the surgeon and her two assistants while we listened to music. At the end of the operation the surgeon found that my blood wasn't flowing as it should and said that the operation hadn't worked. We were all disappointed. My puny veins had let us all down.

I was sent home to recuperate from the operation and was told they would call me in after about three months to have an operation under general anaesthetic to create a fistula graft, which meant inserting a tube into my arm from elbow to shoulder, to enable a good blood flow that would allow access for when I started dialysis. This duly happened and I had to go back into hospital for that operation. I was put onto the renal ward and had the chance to chat to other patients, some of whom were on dialysis and some who'd had kidney transplants. During my time there I realised that dialysis would take up the best part of a week, the three days while it was happening and then the day after each procedure to recover, leaving just one "normal" day. I vowed I would delay dialysis for as long as possible.

The second operation worked but I developed a lump just above my elbow which seemed to be growing. After a few weeks my husband took a photo of this lump and we sent it to the renal department and eventually they called me in to see their vascular surgeon. By this time it looked like a small egg at the elbow joint. The vascular surgeon took one look at it and pronounced, "You have a pseudo-aneurysm there." I said I didn't like the sound of that and he agreed and said it needed to be operated on as an emergency as otherwise, if I knocked it, it could cause fatal bleeding. They took me back into hospital. There were no free slots in the operating theatres so I had to wait, nil by mouth, for four days until a slot became available. Each day I wasn't allowed to eat or drink anything until the evening, by which time it was assumed I wouldn't be able to have the operation that day, and they then gave me some food. It often wasn't much as it was after the last meal and had to be gluten-free. Consequently I lost another 7lbs during those few days. Funnily enough I didn't feel hungry at all.

At last, on the Friday morning they announced I would have the operation that day and so it happened. Later the surgeon came round and showed me some photos of what they had removed. It looked like a large red tennis ball. I was only fearful that it might interfere with the fistula graft but thankfully that remained in good working order. I went home to recover once again.

Once home I was determined to stave off dialysis and read a great deal about kidneys, how they function and how best to protect them. I made a concerted effort to eat a kidney-friendly diet, as well as a gluten-free one, and these two are not necessarily compatible. My best food friends became hummus, red peppers, ginger tea and manuka honey.

That was in the summer of 2020 and continued until the spring of 2021. Since then I have kept off dialysis and have managed to push my kidney function from 8% up to 16%, sometimes 18%. I intend to keep it that way if possible.

I would like to see that young doctor who told me I wasn't going anywhere and seemed willing to push me onto a scrap heap. I would say: "Look at me now. Since your gloomy prognosis I have travelled to Iceland, Sweden, Norway, Germany, Denmark and Lithuania and am about to embark on a holiday to N. America and Canada." If some young doctor writes you off then please prove them wrong.

7. Doing The Ironing

I used to do a lot of ironing. When the boys were still at school I used to iron fifteen shirts a week. That was on top of the usual mixture of trousers, T-shirts, blouses, skirts, dresses, tea-towels, duvet covers, pillowcases and tablecloths. I stopped short of knickers though. I felt that was overdoing it. I have friends who iron their knickers but I felt that knowing they were washed and clean was sufficient. When Dad and Flora came to live with us after Mum died the ironing load increased. Flora had been doing it for a while but it was really too dangerous to allow her to continue as she had Alzheimer's.

Once a week I would disappear into the kitchen to tackle the ironing. Dad was usually sitting in the living room either watching television or reading the paper. Inevitably, after a few minutes, he would potter into the kitchen, sit down and we would chat interspersed with him criticising how I was doing the ironing. To deflect him from this I would question him about his childhood and how he'd met Mum and any interesting family stories. I gleaned a huge amount of information from these conversations. It was a bit like "Who Do You Think You Are?" over the ironing board.

I learnt that as a child he had lived with his parents and six siblings in Diggon Street in London before they moved to Lucas Street. He hadn't particularly enjoyed school as he wasn't academic and he often referred to the fact that he'd only had "an elementary education". He left school at 14 to go out to work. Despite this he had elegant handwriting and was perfectly numerate and literate. He was artistic and started his working life as an embroiderer in a dress factory. That was how he met my mother. She had been widowed young when her daughter, Flora, was just three months old. She'd had to go back to work full time leaving Flora to be brought up by her own mother and sisters when she went back to live with them. She was the oldest of five sisters and two brothers. At the end of the war in 1945, when Flora was five, she decided to send her to boarding school as the best way of letting her mix with other children and be looked after as her mother had said she no longer wanted to be responsible for looking after a young child.

Some of her sisters had married and left home so it was all too much for her mother now.

After the war Mum, who was a dress designer, designed a dress which had two Scottie dogs embroidered on the collar. She needed an embroiderer to do this work and a friend recommended my father. He came to where she was working to discuss this dress and that was how they met. They worked together and began a relationship. My father met Flora and after going out with my mother for some time he said to her one day: "Wouldn't you like Flora to have a younger brother or sister?" That was his marriage proposal which she accepted. They married in 1947 and went on a honeymoon to Switzerland.

There was never much money despite them both working very hard. They set up a small business together, my mother being the designer and also the business brains of a small dress manufacturing company, Sherry Gowns. She allowed one of my Dad's brothers to join them to help out in whichever way he could. They never really hit it off together but she kept her head down and did most of the hard work. Dad helped out with driving, delivering, making sure all the accessories were in order and taking charge of the financial side of things. At the start of their marriage they lived with Mum's mother as they couldn't afford a place of their own and she had the room. He had a hard act to follow as Mum had been a young widow and her late husband achieved saintlike status with some of her siblings and mother due to his early demise. He could never really fill the shoes of someone idealised by those who had only known him for two or three years.

One evening Mum and her mother had a terrible row which culminated with them leaving her house. They went to one of Mum's sisters who took them in for a while until they found a flat of their own to rent. He told me that Mum and her mother didn't speak to each other for a number of years which is why I have no memories of my grandmother from when I was a small child. She came back into our lives when I was about five but she and Dad never had a close relationship. They tolerated each other for Mum's sake.

Dad did his best to be a good father to Flora, legally adopting her as soon as they were married so that she had the same surname. He was the only father that she had ever known and she always tried to please him.

He told me that Mum enriched his life in so many ways. He would never have travelled without her encouragement. He didn't like flying so the few times we went abroad when I was a child we would drive down to Dover, take the ferry across to Calais and then the Golden Arrow train to the South of France. I remember those journeys as being very glamorous and exciting. In later years he and Mum went on a few cruises and he enjoyed those and they saw places they would never have visited otherwise due to his fear of flying.

Mum was very forward thinking and introduced innovations in their work that he would have been reluctant to embrace. She saw the potential for new machinery and new materials and persuaded him to invest in these so their factory kept pace with the modern world. She would look through fashion magazines to see what all the latest trends were and would then incorporate them into her own designs as far as possible. She introduced Flora and I to tights long before any of our friends wore them. They were still stuck with stockings and uncomfortable suspender belts.

He told me stories of when they were courting; how he once bought her a box of chocolates which she left on the back seat of the car and he sat on them without realising. Some of the chocolate melted and stuck to his jacket. He would have been furious if anyone else had let that happen but because it was Mum he never even told her about it and just cleaned his jacket once he was home. Any presents he bought her she used to bring home to share with her younger siblings.

If it wasn't for Dad telling me, I would never have known that Mum arranged for a nest egg to be given to her brother when he came home after the war to enable him to start his own business. She put away some money each week into a savings account for him and insisted that each of her sisters who were working did the same. When he was demobbed he was able to start his own business right away, selling army surplus, because his sister had had the foresight to ensure that he was able to start work as soon as he was out of the army. She also arranged and paid for her youngest brother's Bar Mitzvah as she was living with her mother and her two young-est siblings at the time and her mother couldn't really afford it otherwise. She also helped him in many ways when he started work, also as a dress designer, and taught him all that she knew from her own experience.

It was clear that my father not only loved my mother but looked up to her and admired her. She was his inspiration and his raison d'etre. Those sessions at the ironing board, listening to him recounting their early days together, allowed me to have a deeper understanding of their relationship and of my mother's personality.

I don't do much ironing these days except on an ad hoc basis and only if strictly necessary.

8. Cruising

Our first cruise was to the Norwegian fjords and it was breathtakingly beautiful. It was quite a small ship and we enjoyed the cruise and decided to do more cruising in the future. Our next cruise was to Alaska. It was on a larger ship and the first evening when we went into dinner we met our dinner companions for the first time. On this cruise one sat at the same table with the same people each evening so it would have been a bit unfortunate if we hadn't liked the other people but as it turned out we all liked each other and looked forward to our evening chats.

On the first evening we all introduced ourselves. There were eight of us. As we started eating one of the women, Kiki, said that she did psychometry. One of the others asked what that was and she explained that she could hold some personal object belonging to that person, such as a ring or a watch, and tell them about themselves from it. The man looked contemptuous and said, "I don't believe in such nonsense."

She smiled and said, "Give me your ring please."

He took off his wedding ring and handed it to her. She held it for a few seconds and then stretched across the table, took my hand and pressed the ring into it. "Actually, I'm giving this to you as you'll be much better at it."

I was dumbfounded. "But I've never done anything like that," I protested. She just smiled and closed my hand around the ring. I sat there feeling foolish but then said to the man, "I feel something about painting."

His wife smiled and said, "Well, he's promised to redecorate when we get home." He gave a stiff smile.

After another minute or so I asked, "And who is Vera?"

Both he and his wife put down their knives and forks and he said, very quietly, "Vera was my late mother's name." I handed him back his ring.

Kiki said, "I told you so."

On our way back to our cabin later my husband said, "How did you know about Vera?"

"I've no idea. Her name just came into my head." Kiki told me that when she first saw me she could see I had a dark blue aura and she knew I'd be able to pick things up. I'm still not sure how I feel about that.

Over the next few years we went on other cruises; The Baltic, The Panama Canal, Singapore, Australia and Japan and North America and Canada. They have all been memorable and interesting. There is something so relaxing about watching the sea all around you as you sail smoothly through it with occasional glimpses of whales or dolphins or flying fish. You are cossetted from the moment you're on board and have nothing else to worry or think about except the next stop and what you might be having for dinner. There are talks to listen to, shows to watch in the evening, quizzes and activities throughout the day and bridge to play if you feel so inclined. There are art classes, craft classes, a gym, beauty treatments, massages, a swimming pool, a shop, a library and plenty of other people to chat to and plentiful lounges if you just want to sit and watch or read.

On one of our cruises there were two sisters, identical twins. They not only looked identical but they also dressed identically. It was rather weird actually. They must have been in their 70s or possibly even 80s but always wore the same clothes. They shared a table for two at dinner and although they dressed up in the evenings, it was always still the same evening wear. They even had matching hair slides as they wore their hair in a very 50's little girls' style, with a lock of hair clipped back with a slide. Naturally they lived together and I speculated on how they had been brought up so that they never managed to individualise. They must have had some money to be able to afford to go on cruises so I imagined it must have been inherited money.

The very first cruise I went on was when I was 22 and was engaged to a man I didn't love. The cruise had been arranged before the engagement. I'd booked it with my sister as we often went on holiday together. When I became engaged I didn't feel it was right to cancel the holiday and my fiancé understood the situation. I could never quite work out how I had become engaged to him except to say that he was quite a controlling personality and as he had lost his father a few months beforehand, I felt obliged to go on seeing him. On the cruise, which was to Norway, we met a couple of young men who were travelling together. They were both solicitors and worked together. One of them took an interest in me and we chatted together.

One evening after dinner we both went up on deck and were looking at the night sky. He suddenly took my left hand and held it up and looked at the solitaire diamond ring on my finger.

"So, what's this then?" he asked.

"It's an engagement ring," I replied.

"Yes, I know that," he said. "When are you getting married?"

"I don't know. We haven't set a date yet."

He looked at me and I felt myself blush. I looked up at the inky black sky shot with silver stars and the vast expanse of dark water surrounding us. He pulled me towards him and kissed me. The kiss went on for a long time and I closed my eyes. His hand was cradled round my head. Eventually he let me go and I opened my eyes and started to cry. He said softly, "I don't think you want to marry him, do you?"

"No," I said. "I never wanted to get engaged but somehow couldn't get out of it."

"What are you going to do?" he asked.

I knew from the way I had responded to his kiss that I could never go ahead with this intended marriage. It would be a disaster. "I'll finish it when we get home."

"Make sure you do," he said.

On the last day of the cruise I sat in our cabin and wrote a letter to my fiancé's mother explaining why I was breaking off our engagement. I knew that by doing it that way then I would have no excuse not to go ahead with telling him as his mother would have already received the letter. When we were back home I posted the letter and the next day told him. I gave him back his ring. He was not at all happy about my decision but I was resolved. We parted ways although it took me some months to extricate myself fully.

It was many years before I went on another cruise and then it was again to the Norwegian fjords. This time it was with my husband and it was a beautiful experience. The fjords are every bit as beautiful as their many glorious photos promise. We shared a table with a group of fun-loving ladies from a bowling club who made each meal a pleasurable occasion. There was much laughter and light-hearted chatter. It was a deeply enjoyable holiday with wonderful scenery and whetted our appetite for cruising.

Since then we have cruised down the Panama Canal, been all round the Mediterranean, been to Iceland, Singapore, Australia and New Zealand as well as Japan and the Baltic. Every time it has been a pleasure. Our last cruise was to North America and Canada. We're deciding where we can go next.

9. House Hunting

If you've ever sold one property and bought another then you will know that it is quite a stressful experience. Imagine selling two properties to buy one. That takes things to another level. We embarked on this mission so as to enable my father and sister to come and live with us. We lived in a three-bedroomed semi with our two teenage sons, one of whom was in his first year at university. My father and sister lived in a flat about a 20 minute drive away but they were both in ill health and needed looking after. I was running our two households but it was becoming impossible. One evening my father rang to say that my sister had flooded their bathroom, again, and we had to go over there to sort things out. On the way home my husband said, "They can't go on like this." And I had to agree. He suggested that we all live together so that I could look after them properly and it would be easier if we were in the same house. I asked how we could do that given the present circumstances. He said that we'd have to sell both our properties and buy one house suitable for us all. That's how it all began.

For every four houses that we looked at we took my father and sister to see one as I knew that one or both of them wouldn't like certain ones. It was a long and laborious process. During the year in which it took to find the right place we viewed many properties. Some of them were memorable. One of the first ones we saw was a pleasant four-bedroomed house in a leafy road, near to shops and a station. When we arrived the lady of the house showed us round. When we came to the living room there were ten large black and white photographs arranged on the walls. Each one was of the lady of the house, naked, in each month of a pregnancy, the last one being of her holding a new-born baby. I wasn't phased by them but I could see that my husband looked most uncomfortable, particularly as the woman was now in front of us showing us round, albeit fully clothed. We didn't take my father and sister to view this house.

Another house that we both liked we decided we could take my father and sister to see. I arranged with the estate agent for us to view the house while the owners were at work. The estate agent met us outside.

64

He had the keys to the house and opened the door to let us in. We started to look at the downstairs. When we came to the kitchen he opened the door and immediately a small dog, I think it was a terrier of some kind, flew out of the kitchen like a bullet and ran to the front door which the agent had left ajar for some reason. The dog ran out of the door and up the street. The agent looked appalled and ran after him. We stood in the hall and watched. It was like a scene from some comedy film as the estate agent ran after the dog who leapt into front gardens and ran around up driveways then back onto the street. The chase lasted for about 10 minutes until eventually the dog came to a stop at something that proved irresistibly alluring. He was sniffing around this when the estate agent, puffing and red-faced, picked him up and carried him back to the house. He didn't say a word but put him back in the kitchen and closed the door behind him. He turned to us and said, "I'm really sorry about that. I had no idea there was a dog in there." We smiled understandingly and looked at the rest of the house. It wasn't the one we went for.

We saw many houses that we liked which my father then vetoed on all kinds of grounds. One was a beautiful house with a magnificent garden at the end of a cul-de-sac. The main living room and three bedrooms and a bathroom were all on the ground floor. It had a large kitchen overlooking the garden. There was an upstairs but you had to go up a spiral staircase to reach it. The upstairs had a large main bedroom with an en-suite bathroom. We really liked this house and were happy with the layout. When we took them to see it my father looked at the spiral staircase and said, "I could never get up there." And we agreed but said it wasn't a problem as that would be our bedroom. He wouldn't hear of it though so we had to abandon the idea of that house.

One of the funniest moments happened when I came with my father and sister for a viewing of a house that we had liked. We arranged with the estate agent for him to meet us outside and he would show us round as the owners were at work. I collected my father and sister and we arrived at the house at 9 a.m. as arranged. The estate agent let us in and we started looking downstairs. Once we'd looked at the downstairs I started to go up the stairs and knew that the first room on the right at the top of the stairs was a bathroom. I opened the door to this bathroom and was startled to find a man sitting in the bath. He looked as startled as I did. I said, "I'm terribly sorry," and closed the door again. I turned round as the others were trooping up the stairs.

I said, "There's a man in the bath" and the estate agent stopped and said, "No. The owners are supposed to be out."

"Well one of them isn't as he's in the bath," I said. Everyone turned round and went back down again. That was another house we didn't go for.

We did eventually find a house that we were all happy with. It was on a new estate of 14 houses and we saw the show house which we then took my father and sister to see. My father loved it as it was so new and clean and uncluttered. I'd seen the plans for the houses and knew that the show house was not quite right for us but there was one other house, not yet built, which I knew would be perfect. It had a straight staircase which would be ideal for the stair-lift that I knew we would have to have fitted for my father fairly soon. The design upstairs was very simple with a square hall and the four bedrooms round it, nothing complicated so it would be easy for my sister to negotiate.

We had to wait a few more months for this house to be completed but we made regular visits to it to watch its progress. We finally completed our sale two weeks before my father completed his sale so we were able to move in and get things a little organised before they joined us. Our house-hunting days were over.

10. School Days

My first experience of school was when I was three. I was sent to a small nursery school in Devonshire Street. My memories of it are vague but I do recall walking up a large staircase to a main room. There was a smell of boiled cabbage. The school was run by two sisters and catered for rather upper-class children. I mixed with little lords, ladies and other honourables. We used to go for walks in Regent's Park and would walk there in crocodile fashion, each child holding the coat tail of the child in front. After lunch each day we would be put to sleep, sharing in double beds, each bed with a large soft toy on it. One of my earliest memories is of having a struggle with the child I shared the bed with as we each wanted to cuddle the soft toy. We both pulled at it and the poor thing split in half. We hastily tucked it down the bottom of the bed under the mattress and I recall feeling heavily burdened with guilt for the next 24 hours but nothing happened. I also remember doing jigsaw puzzles and being read to and colouring in. My mother would collect me at the end of each day, as opposed to most of the other children who were collected by their uniformed nannies. We would then travel home on the tube from Baker Street station.

When I was almost five I started Wessex Gardens Primary School, which was situated along the Hendon Way. I went to both the Infants and the Junior School there. I don't remember much about the Infants but the Junior School was a time when we were all being prepared for the 11+. Luckily my parents didn't put any pressure on me regarding these important exams as I knew that some of my classmates were bribed with promises of bicycles or other goodies if they passed. I always remember an art teacher called Mrs Solway who fostered my love of drawing and painting and would be enthusiastic in her praise of my efforts. In the third and fourth years leading up to the 11+ we had the same teacher, Mrs Miller, who was determined that her entire class would pass the exam. We were relentlessly drilled in our times tables and spellings and each week she gave us a mock exam to complete. Every week we had to write an essay and complete numerous maths questions. I struggled with maths but the constant repetition of times tables and numerous examples of multiplication and long division ensured that I reached an adequate standard in arithmetic. English was never a problem and we were given a spelling test every Friday with a list of words to learn every Monday in preparation for this. The third exam was more general and tested ability in various areas. We were given old exam papers to practise our skills.

Although we all had to work hard to achieve good results there was still time for other activities. I particularly enjoyed art lessons and let my imagination run free painting exotic multi-coloured creatures and dream landscapes. I also enjoyed drawing people and although we had no formal lessons in life drawing I used to draw the other children in the class and practised doing things like hands or faces.

One of our other lessons was needlework. I think the boys were taken elsewhere to do woodwork. I remember our last year in school all the girls had to embroider a sampler. This consisted of a large piece of material with tiny holes in it and we had to embroider neat lines in different stitches; cross-stitch, blanket stitch, chain stitch, double cross stitch and some I don't recall. After doing about a dozen lines in different colours of these various embroidery stitches we then had to embroider our names. I remember walking up to Mrs Miller's desk where she had the beautiful embroidery silks laid out and we could choose which colours we wanted to use. The colours were jewel bright and enticing. I used to hover over the emerald green and sapphire blue, amber gold and shimmering scarlet. I looked forward to these lessons and also used to love having a story read to us on a Friday afternoon. This was a special end to the working week which I think Mrs Miller introduced as a way of winding us down ready for the weekend.

I remember the two days of the 11+ exam because both my parents were working so no one would be home by the time I finished the exams which always took place in the morning. It was arranged that I would take the bus to near where one of my aunts lived and she would meet me at the bus stop and take me home for the afternoon so my parents could collect me on their way home from work. This particular aunt had three children, the oldest of whom I used to play with regularly. She was six months younger than me so was in the year below me at

72

school. My aunt was very keen to hear all about the exams and after she'd given us all lunch she insisted I go upstairs and have a sleep on my cousin's bed. I found this strange as I wasn't used to being sent up to sleep in the afternoon but did as I was told. I lay on the bed and listened to my cousins playing out in the garden. I didn't sleep but just lay there quietly until my aunt came up to say I'd rested long enough. My parents didn't ask much about the exams. Apparently when the letter arrived informing them that I'd passed my father was extremely surprised. He never thought I was particularly bright and was really taken aback that I'd passed the 11+.

Then came the decision as to which secondary school I should attend. My sister, who was seven years older than me, had won a scholarship to Godolphin & Latymer when she was 11. We lived in Osterley at that time so it was a fairly easy journey for her to go on the train to Hammersmith. When she was 12 we moved and her journey would have been much too difficult so my mother wrote to the local education board asking for advice. They said she could attend the Henrietta Barnett School which was much nearer to us. She was delighted as she hated it at Godolphin

& Latymer and was much happier at the Hen Barn as we called it. As she was seven years older than me she was in her final year when I came for my interview.

My mother was too busy to come with me to the interview so my father accompanied me. I was the only girl in the waiting room with her father rather than her mother. In the interview I had to read an extract from *Silas Marner* and answer some questions about it and then tell the headmistress a bit about myself. It wasn't a long interview and afterwards my sister collected me and took me back to the prefects' room (she was a prefect) and gave me a chocolate biscuit while the other prefects asked me about the interview.

By the time I started the school in September she had gone on to higher education but she left a long shadow. As soon as I gave my name to each new teacher they immediately asked if she was my sister so she had set a difficult precedent, being both clever and popular. I couldn't live up to her high standards but I tried my best.

The bane of my life was needlework. How I longed for the happy days of embroidering with beautiful coloured silks in a sun-dappled classroom. Our needlework teacher was a terrifying woman who lived in a classroom at the top of a winding staircase. She was large and had spectacles perched on the end of her nose. She wore hand-knitted sweaters in varying shades of sludge. I couldn't get to grips with the sewing machine. The intricacies of threading the needle totally eluded me and each time I had to ask for help just to get going. My sewing on it was erratic at best. I couldn't wait for the six months of needlework to end. We then had six months of domestic science with the same teacher. I fared somewhat better here, although in our first lesson we had to make blancmange, something I loathed. Even writing the name makes me feel nauseous. I tipped the whole pink, milky mess down the toilet as soon as I could. I watched it flush away with a huge sigh of relief. Our next culinary effort was a Victoria sponge sandwich. This turned out much better. I found I actually enjoyed creaming the sugar and butter together, sifting in the flour, adding the eggs and smoothing the batter into a cake tin. I was delighted when I brought the finished product out of the oven. It had risen, was smooth and golden on top, slightly domed, and once filled with jam and dusted with icing sugar was wonderfully edible. I took it home with some triumph. We then learnt some of the basics of simple cookery, lessons which have stayed with me.

The second bane of my life was hockey. This was a game I found to be quite inexplicable. How could anyone enjoy shivering on a wet, muddy field, one's legs encased in scratchy knee pads and wielding a large curved wooden stick. The point of the game seemed pointless to me so I skulked around the edges of the playing field trying to keep out of everyone's way. Netball was a slight improvement. At least I had the advantage of height and a good eye so could usually manage to lob the ball into the net. The team captain soon noticed that and picked me for her team.

We also had to do deportment classes, where we walked around the gym in threes while being scrutinised by the gym teacher. Anyone found wanting in the way they walked or stood was sent for remedial lessons. Fortunately I wasn't one of those.

During our first year we also had one lesson a week called "speech training". This was taken by a white-haired lady who questioned us all in the first lesson as we each stood in turn and spoke about ourselves for a couple of minutes. After my introduction she said, somewhat sneeringly, "And how long have you been having elocution lessons?" I was surprised and answered, "I've never had an elocution lesson in my life." She sniffed and looked at me as though I'd been telling lies but moved on to the next girl.

Our days were filled with maths, English, French, history, geography, science, art, gym lessons, religious instruction and singing. We were given hours of homework each day. The school was situated at the top of a hill overlooking Central Square in the Hampstead Garden Suburb. There were no bus routes so whichever direction you came from there was a long walk to get to school. Mine involved walking up Hoop Lane with the crematorium on one side and a cemetery on the other. I'm sure all that walking was good for us.

The next seven years passed swiftly as we were kept so busy. We emerged into the bright light of day having acquired a number of GCEs and some "A" levels to go on to whatever we were doing next. So, school was over. My education then began.

11. The Wedding Dress

Late night shopping was on a Thursday and I decided it was time to go looking for my wedding dress. It was early January and our wedding was booked for early April. Nowadays that wouldn't be enough time but back then it seemed plenty of time. I finished work at 5.30 p.m. so had about two and half hours in which to find the dress.

The irony of it was that my mother was a dressmaker and could easily have made my dress but she had no time. She'd made wedding dresses and bridesmaid dresses for many family members and friends but at this time in her life she was busy running her own factory and was permanently frazzled. She didn't even have time to accompany me on this shopping trip so I went alone.

Over the years my mother had made many of my clothes. When I was very small she used to make me practical dungarees which I wore with different tops underneath. This was at a time when most little girls wore puffed sleeve dresses with smocking and sashes. She was way ahead of her time. As a child she used to make me pinafore dresses in serviceable materials which, again, I would wear with different tops underneath. She also made slightly more fancy dresses which I wore to parties or when going out. I did have one shop bought dress which I liked very much. It was a black watch tartan with a white Peter Pan collar with a red bow in the middle of the collar. I was sad when I outgrew that dress. My mother often made me clothes out of "cabbage", the off-cuts from material she'd used to make dresses. There was one I particularly remember which was a white piqué patterned with blue roses. For a friend's 12th birthday party she made a simple A-line dress in a pale pink fabric. It was much admired. Before one summer holiday she made me four new dresses, all to the same pattern, which I wore in rotation throughout that summer. They were all sleeveless, plain shift dresses and I alternated them with two summer skirts, also made from "cabbage".

When I embarked on this shopping expedition I didn't have as much experience as maybe some other young women might have had. I did have enthusiasm though and the novelty of the occasion. I started my search at a shop that specialised in bridalwear. It was on two floors and the downstairs had an array of bridesmaid dresses and mother-of-the-bride outfits. I went up to the second floor which was exclusively for wedding dresses. As I reached the top of the stairs I heard a young woman saying, "I think it needs more flowers on it." She was wearing a voluminous dress which had tiny pink and blue flowers embroidered around the neckline. The skirt had more flowers scattered on it, each one with a little crystal in the centre. She had an entourage of three friends and an older woman who I guessed was her mother. They were scrutinising the dress and her mother said, "I think it has enough flowers, darling." Her friends kept quiet.

I walked past them to the end of the room to start looking at the many racks of dresses on display. I was somewhat overwhelmed at the sheer number of dresses and how much variety there was on the theme of a long white dress.

I picked out three dresses to try on. They were all very different so that I might decide which style I preferred. The first one had a fullish skirt but not the whole ballgown look. It was satin with a delicate design all over, accentuated by tiny seed pearls. Once I had it on it felt extremely heavy and I couldn't imagine wearing it for a whole day, or near enough a whole day. It looked pretty enough but didn't give me any kind of thrill. I took it off and put it back on the rail. The second dress was very delicate, in chiffon, a bit Grecian looking. The bodice was in a crossover style and the skirt flowed in folds. I looked at myself in the mirror and decided it looked more like an elaborate nightgown than a wedding dress. It went back on the rail. The third dress was slimmer-fitting. It had a sweetheart neckline and a little diamante belt accentuating the waist. The skirt was neither too full nor too tight. I twirled around a couple of times but, again, it didn't make my heart beat any faster and I thought it just didn't have that "je ne sais quoi". Reluctantly I put that one back too. I quickly looked through the rest of the dresses in my size but nothing stood out. I left that shop and decided to go to a large department store instead.

This one had a bridal department on the second floor so I made my way up there and realised that I'd already spent an hour on this quest. The choice here was much smaller but I found two dresses that I liked. One was lace. It was slim fitting with long sleeves. I liked it but it wasn't anything particularly special. It looked like many wedding dresses I'd seen on other brides. It was a safe choice. The other one was in a fine fabric with a delicate pattern of what looked like fans all over it. The skirt was in three tiers overlapping each other. There was a deep frill round the neckline that came over the shoulders. I liked it and it was a bit more unusual than the others I'd tried. I wished I had someone with me to give their opinion. There was another young woman also trying on dresses. We each disappeared into our cubicles and came out to look at ourselves in the floor length mirror. She had just emerged in a full Cinderella dress, a crinoline in white taffeta. She glanced at me and I said she looked lovely. "It's a bit standard though, isn't it?" she said.

"Well, it is a bit Cinderella princess like, if that's what you mean," I said.

"I'm waiting to feel that 'moment' when you just know it's the right one."

I nodded. "Yes, I know what you mean. I haven't had that moment either."

She looked at the dress I was wearing. "That's a beautiful dress." she said. "Don't you think that's 'the one' for you?"

"I'm not sure," I said. "I liked it on the hanger and I like it on but it doesn't make my heart stop or anything."

"Oh, well you have to go on looking then."

I decided she was right so I wished her good luck and went on my way. The next shop I went into was more of a boutique which only had a small selection of wedding dresses. They were at the far end of the shop and there were about 20 wedding dresses. I carefully went down the rail, picking out one or two to look at more closely. Then I saw it. I nearly missed it as it was almost hidden by two voluminous dresses either side of it. I drew it out and held it up. It was a simple dress with a square neckline, very fitted with a beautifully elegant skirt. There were no embellishments on it and the material was plain. I took it to the dressing room to try it on.

As I zipped it up I felt that it fitted perfectly. It felt smooth and light and supremely comfortable. I came out to look at it in the long mirror. I gasped at my own reflection. I had never seen myself look so regal. It was like something Audrey Hepburn might have worn. I knew it was "the one". It was the most expensive dress I'd ever bought but it was for the most special day in my life so far. I took it to the saleslady who carefully wrapped it in tissue paper and put it into a beautiful bag. She asked me if I wanted to look at veils or shoes. I hadn't thought as far as a veil but said I'd leave the veil for the moment. I did look at shoes though and found the perfect pair. They were completely plain, white satin, with small heels. I bought the shoes as well. On the way home I felt light-hearted and light-headed.

Once home I showed the dress to my mother who thoroughly approved of it. "Let me make the veil," she said.

"All right," I said. "That would be lovely." The following week she brought home a veil. It was very long and plain except that she'd trimmed the edge with a slightly translucent material so that it gave off a slight sheen as I moved. It complemented the dress perfectly. I was now ready for my wedding.

12. Temping

When I first started going out to work I signed up with an employment agency to do "temping" as a way to gain experience and to decide where I wanted to work. I continued temping for nearly three years. At that time, in the 60s, many firms employed "temps" on a regular basis and I was never short of a job. One of the first jobs I was sent to was for the editor of a small magazine based near Oxford Street in London. This magazine specialised in mothers and babies and was housed in the same block as various other magazines, all just occupying one room on each floor. One was aimed at teenage girls and another at young men, called *Health and Efficiency* and featured body builders and tips on how to keep fit. There were many young models, both male and female, and pop stars coming in and out.

The work was not particularly inspiring and my boss was often out of the office. She told me that one of her previous secretaries was Angela Carter who later became the famous writer. I was sent back there week after week and worked there for about three months in total. I gradually realised the reason my boss was out of the office so much was because she was having an affair and her long lunches and absent afternoons were not because she was interviewing someone or working on a particular story. It was because she was meeting her lover. I held the fort but didn't really know what I was doing and felt out of my depth with no one to tell me what to do. When the agency offered me a different placement I decided to try that one instead.

My next job was for The Public Trustee in Sardinia Street near Holborn. That was a revelation as it was just like the offices depicted in some old movies; rows of desks with everyone working diligently and not speaking to anyone else. I was assigned a desk and told I would be working for a particular man who duly came to collect me for dictation. I sat taking his letters for most of the morning and then went to my desk and typed them out during the rest of the day. It was unutterably boring, particularly as the content of the letters was dull as ditchwater. One afternoon when I came back from my lunch break I inadvertently took the lift to the wrong floor, came out, made my way to my desk and only once seated I realised that I was on the wrong floor. Everything looked identical but the work on the desk wasn't the same as I'd been working on before lunch. I left that room and went to the correct room and at the end of the week asked the agency to send me somewhere different the next week.

They then sent me to a shipping company where again I was in a room of other girls typing at their desks. This time I was working for a man with an office overlooking this room and when I went into his room for dictation he sat with his feet up on his desk, just a few inches from my face. He never looked at me or addressed me by name but just rattled through the letters and sent me off to type them. At the end of that week I again asked the agency to send me somewhere different.

I was then sent to a solicitors' office in Blackfriars. It was somewhat Dickensian but at least the office had some character to it and the man I worked for treated me like a human being. He had a heavy workload and we raced through letter after letter. Some of the work involved typing out contracts which were lengthy and tedious but also demanding and needed to be perfect. This was a good preparation for whatever other work I might be offered in the future. I stayed there for three weeks and then requested a change.

I was then sent to a small hospital whose matron needed help in her office. This involved a totally different kind of work. One of the hardest jobs was to complete all the time sheets for the nurses who worked there. Each one left her time sheet on a Monday morning and I had to go through them all, logging every hour the nurse had worked and whether it was a day or night shift and whether it was overtime. It was quite exacting and I had to calculate what each nurse had earned that week. I certainly didn't want to make any mistakes. It became more complicated when some worked extra shifts at different times and their hours differed from week to week. Funnily enough I rather enjoyed working my way through their time sheets, ensuring that my calculations were correct.

Apart from these time sheets, which took the best part of Monday and Tuesday to complete, there were more general letters and lots of telephone calls to make. At the same time I would receive calls from relatives of the patients and also from other doctors, hospitals and funeral directors. It was busy and I found the work rewarding. I stayed there for over six months.

When I decided I needed a change of scene I was sent to another firm of solicitors in Gresham Street in the City of London. This was for a very large firm who employed many "temps" on a regular basis and I was moved from department to department so gained experience in conveyancing, wills, trusts and some litigation. One Monday morning I was sent back to the conveyancing department and started to work for a young man who shared his office with another man, both of whom were ex-public schoolboys. We established a good rapport and I was working in an office with two other secretaries and there was a convivial atmosphere.

The young man I worked for was a great sportsman and used to play a lot of games outside of work, particularly hockey. One morning he hobbled into work obviously in pain due to having injured his feet. He'd forgotten his hockey boots and borrowed someone else's for a match the previous evening and had suffered as a result. He called me in to his room and asked if I could dress his feet to help alleviate the pain he was in. He took his shoes and socks off and put his feet on the desk and I saw how he'd managed to gouge out lumps of flesh. It looked very painful. He'd brought with him antiseptic cream, bandages and plasters so I cleaned his feet, smeared antiseptic cream on them and put plasters on the smaller cuts then bandaged his feet to protect them. I did this every morning for the next two weeks until his feet had healed.

This was only my second experience of working in a legal firm so I wasn't entirely used to the language. One day after I'd taken in some letters for him to sign I heard gales of laughter. I'd been typing a letter about a factory lease and I'd inadvertently transcribed from my shorthand "statues and decorations" instead of "statutes and declarations". He found this highly amusing and I think it rather endeared me to him. I continued to work for him for about six months.

In the office I shared with two other girls, one was a permanent secretary, Carol, who'd been there for years and the other was a temp like me. This third temp changed fairly frequently so every few weeks there'd be a new one. One day a new temp arrived who was a breath of fresh air. She was Australian and was very lively. She kept us both in stitches a lot of the time. One particular morning she came in and said that the night before she'd left her knickers on the floor and in the morning there was a huge spider nestled in them. "I had to give them a real shake-out before putting them on!" she said. Carol and I stared at each other in stunned silence before both collapsing in giggles. Denise, our Australian temp, looked somewhat bemused.

I was fascinated by the fact that both the man I was working for and the colleague who shared his room were ex-public school boys but I realised that in many ways my education had been more thorough than theirs. One day they were discussing the difference between "subjective" and "objective" and they didn't know the difference. I had to explain it to them. Their spelling also left much to be desired. It certainly made me question whether a public school education was money well spent.

I continued to work at this firm for different people over the next few months but then decided I was due another change.

I requested to be sent to another legal firm as I had enjoyed the work and felt I was now quite experienced. One Monday morning I was sent to a much smaller firm in Moorgate. It was quite a Dickensian place with a winding wooden staircase. I arrived at the third floor and waited in the room I was sent to for my new boss to appear. It was a small room, overlooking Moorgate, with two desks next to each other. The other desk was occupied by a blonde lady who was friendly and introduced herself as Christine. She said I would be working for a Mr Williams whose secretary had left some months ago to have a baby and hadn't been replaced permanently as yet.

A few minutes later Mr Williams came in and introduced himself and took me off to his room for dictation. We spent the morning in there while he dictated letter upon letter. I came back just before lunch time and he said I should go to lunch and start typing up the letters in the afternoon. He laughed and said, "Please don't disappear like one girl did a few weeks ago." I reassured him that I would be back in the afternoon. I waded through the mountain of letters without too much trouble and took in a sheaf of letters for him to sign in time for the evening post. He seemed happy with my work and each day we did a similar amount of work including typing up various contracts and wills.

At the end of the week I took my time sheet into him to sign and he did so and then said, "Well, you can't leave me now. Can you please come back next week and stay permanently?"

I thought about it for a few seconds and said, "Yes, of course." That was my first permanent job and I never temped again.

13. Who Do You Think You Are?

My maternal grandmother came to England from a small village outside Kiev at the age of sixteen. Her elder brother persuaded their mother to flee from the pogroms sweeping their country. Her two older sisters were married with young families so they decided to stay. They duly perished.

Ethel arrived in England on a damp, grey, dismal day and hated it immediately. She missed the landscape of Russia and the bright cold and the countryside. She was sent to work in a dress factory, being illiterate and having no other skills other than an ability to sew. It was there that she met her future husband, Isaac, who had also fled Russia to escape to a more tolerant country.

Two years later they were married. Ethel was 18 and Isaac was 20. When Ethel was 19 she had my mother, Sarah, the first of nine children, eight of whom survived to adulthood. Life was tough as they did not have much money and every couple of years Ethel had another baby. It meant that I had five aunties and two uncles on my mother's side of the family. My father was the sixth of seven children so on his side I had five uncles and one auntie. This yielded twenty-two first cousins.

Both my parents worked full time so this large extended family came in extremely useful during school holidays as I would be sent to stay with one of them for a few days or a week at a time. They were my parents' childcare, given freely and with love. I grew up with a close bond to many of my cousins. It also taught me an invaluable lesson in that I discovered early on in life that not all families are run on the same lines.

My Warwick grandmother was very beautiful, as attested to by the two photographs I have seen taken just before or just after she arrived in England. She had high Slavic cheekbones, looked some-what aristocratic, and was wearing a white high-necked Edwardian blouse, a long dark skirt and a wide belt. Her hair was coiled in a long braid round her head. She was unsmiling as was the custom for photographs at that time.

Soon after they married the First World War began and my mother said that her

95

earliest memory was of her father holding her up and sitting her on a ledge in an air raid shelter in one of London's underground stations. She also remembers walking along holding her father's hand while her mother was holding her newly-born baby brother and they were looking for new lodgings because their house had been bombed.

There was little money to spare but her mother made all the children's clothes, a skill she passed on to her oldest daughter. She was also good at eking out the available food. My mother said she would sometimes mash up two bananas and spread it on slices of spread with each child having one slice of bread and mashed banana for their tea. In this way she made two bananas feed eight children. She would also darn their clothes if holes appeared. At school the teacher would often hold up the arm of one child with a neatly darned sleeve saying, "Look how Mrs Warwick looks after her children's clothes." In fact the child often felt embarrassed because the darn would be a completely different colour but it was all that Mrs Warwick had available. They may not have had much money or many material possessions but they had each other so there was always someone to play with and they all looked out for each other. They were a close family and remained so throughout their lives.

My mother recalls that at some time during her childhood her mother suffered from bad headaches and decided it was due to the weight of her long hair. She went to the hairdresser and had her hair cut short. Her father was furious and wouldn't speak to his wife for the next two weeks. It sounded as though they had rather a tempestuous marriage as they both had fiery tempers but the fires were short-lived and they had a long marriage until my grandfather's death from cancer when my mother was 28. This meant that my sister also lost her surrogate father at the age of three.

The sisters were always close and my mother, as the oldest, was the one who kept them all together. If she ever heard of any disagreement or feud she would intervene and invite each of the aggrieved parties to come over for a cup of tea, air their grievances and iron matters out. No one was allowed to fall out with one of their siblings.

I also used to stay with my paternal grandmother during the holidays, usually for one week at a time. She had come to

England in the early 1900s, recently married but with not a word of English. She had been born into a farming family in Romania and told me stories of her life as a child where she would swim in the local river, ride horses and be taught by her mother how to make butter and cheese. It must have been a shock to arrive in Hull in England, also escaping from a perilous situation in her own country.

She could neither read nor write and was also innumerate and yet was a wonderful cook. She must have carried all her recipes in her head and never used precise measurements just using spoonfuls or cupfuls instead. Despite this her cakes were always magnificent and her meals were legendary. I remember standing and watching her making a delicacy called verunikas, which were a bit reminiscent of Italian ravioli. She would roll out the pastry very thinly, then cut it into little diamond shapes and fill each one with a mixture of mashed potato and caramelized onion, then fold them up into little crescent-shaped parcels before cooking them. They were delicious. When all her children were adults she would bake seven cakes every Friday and each of her sons would come in to see her on their way home and collect one of her freshly baked cakes for the weekend.

My mother's family lived in a flat above a pub in Globe Road in London and my mother was the only one to have a room on her own, her five sisters sharing two other rooms. She told me that as a child she would regularly wake in the night and see two women wrestling at the end of her bed. They were dressed in Victorian clothes. They didn't frighten her in any way. She was just curious and often wondered about the history of the place they were living in.

My mother was academically gifted and one year won a prize for a short story she'd written. When it was time to collect her prize she had already left school as she had to leave at 14 to go out to work and help contribute towards her keep. One of her younger sisters went to collect it in her place and it was given to her by the late Queen Mary. There was a Warwick in every class at their local school. Most of her younger sisters were also clever but each of them had to leave school at 14 to go out and work. There was no question of any of them going on to higher education.

Their father had been taught by a tutor back home in Russia and was a cultured man but had to take a lowly job once in

England. He loved the opera and used to go regularly, standing at the back as that was all he could afford. He nurtured a love of learning in his children and my mother was an avid reader throughout her life. She also enjoyed the theatre and concerts.

My mother married at the age of 25 in 1939, little knowing that in less than two years she would be a widow with a three-month-old baby. She and my sister went back to live with her mother and my sister's early life was deeply traumatic but that is another story.*

Her own sisters' adolescence was spent during the war years so once the war had ended they embraced life with gusto and most of them married in 1947. My mother herself also re-married in 1947, having met her second husband at work during the war years.

She told me a story of when her sisters were still children and she had just started work. She decided to take two of them to the pantomime one Christmas but could only afford standing only places. The three of them were standing at the back of the stalls, excitedly waiting for the pantomime to begin, when an older couple approached them to ask if the two little girls might like to sit in a spare seat they had as their grand-daughter was unable to accompany them due to being ill. My mother accepted for them and they duly went and squeezed in together on the spare seat. The lady asked them their names and Auntie Freda, being the elder of the two, said, "I'm Freda Warwick and this is my sister, Bella Warwick." The lady sounded interested and said "Oh, might you be related to the Warwicks of..." Auntie Freda didn't know who she was talking about so she replied, "No, we're the Warwicks of Bethnal Green."

* The story of my sister, who was diagnosed with early-onset Alzheimer's at the age of 54, is told in my previous book, *Soul Stories – How Attachment Shapes Our Lives*, published in 2020.

14. The Girl From The Mountains

Sofia was the third of five daughters born to a Greek peasant farmer and his wife. They lived high up in a mountainous region and he worked hard on his small farm where he had some goats as well as almond and fig trees. Sofia helped out from an early age, as did her two older sisters. She also helped her mother with her two younger siblings and with the cooking and housework. She started at the local village school when she was six and it was soon clear that she was academically gifted. She learned to read and write quickly and was also good at mathematics. She absorbed learning like a hungry sponge.

The family lived in a small cottage which only had three rooms and a kitchen. She and her sisters shared one bedroom, her parents had another and there was one living room. They washed outside with water from a well and there was an outside toilet. Life was hard but they loved each other and always had food to eat, even if it was often repetitive like goats' cheese and olives. They swapped produce with other farmers who lived nearby so they always had fresh fruits and vegetables. Sometimes her father would go into the nearest town, borrowing his neighbour's donkey to do so. He would come home with fish from the market and other foods they couldn't supply themselves.

Sofia's mother had a younger sister who lived in Athens. She was married to a wealthy man, a lawyer, and they lived in a large house. They didn't have any children and after ten years of marriage it seemed that they couldn't have children. Sofia's aunt sometimes came to visit them for a day and when Sofia was seven her mother and aunt decided, at her aunt's suggestion, that she should go and live with her aunt in Athens. This would enable her to have a better education and a better standard of living all round and would give her family more room in the cottage. It was arranged that she would return home for six weeks in the summer and for one week at Easter and Christmas. She was not involved in this discussion but it was put to her on one of her aunt's visits and that same day she duly went back with her aunt to Athens. She said goodbye to her sisters and parents and left with a small bag packed with her few belongings. There was hardly any time for her to process what was going on or to understand the impact it might have on her. She was excited to be going to Athens for the first time and she had become fond of her aunt on her occasional visits as she always brought lovely presents for the girls and was affectionate towards them.

They arrived in Athens in the late evening so Sofia met her uncle and was given something to eat and then put to bed. She had her own bedroom which had two large windows overlooking a pretty square with trees surrounding it. The next day her aunt took her shopping and bought her some new dresses and two pairs of shoes. She had been used to going barefoot much of the time but did own one pair of sandals. She also bought her some pretty nightdresses and more underwear. She was thrilled with all of these purchases as she was used to wearing hand-me down clothes from her two older sisters. In the afternoon her aunt enrolled her at the local school and also bought her a new pencil case with a good supply of pencils to go in it, both lead ones and coloured ones.

Her aunt's house seemed like a mansion to Sofia but it only took her a few days to become used to it. She was also overwhelmed by the food she was given, much of it so luxurious that she had never tasted before like ice cream, pastries and all kinds of meats and fish that she didn't even know existed. Each morning her aunt made her a proper breakfast and in the evenings she sat with her aunt and uncle in their large dining room for their dinner. At lunchtime she sat in the kitchen with her aunt who made a simple meal but it was still more plentiful and varied than what she was used to eating at home.

She had arrived on a Thursday, Friday had been busy shopping and then there was the weekend. On the Monday morning her aunt walked with her to her new school and she was introduced to the class. To her delight she found that she could keep up quite easily with everything they were learning. In fact in some things she was more advanced and her teachers soon realised that she was a girl of outstanding ability. She enjoyed her schoolwork and soon made friends with some of the other girls.

Her life in Athens soon settled into a comfortable routine although each night when she went to bed she missed the scent of the mountain air and the sounds of the goats bleating. She also missed her sisters and her parents but thought to herself how lucky she was to have everything else that she now had in her life. She knew that many girls would have envied her new lifestyle.

A few months after arriving in Athens her aunt discovered, to her astonishment and almost disbelief, that she was pregnant. At first she thought it a mistake and that she had miscalculated when her last period was but after two months she knew it had to be, particularly as she felt sick each morning and her breasts felt larger and uncomfortable. She went to the doctor who confirmed that she was indeed pregnant. There was great joy in the household and her aunt and uncle made much of Sofia, believing it was her presence that had achieved what they both thought was impossible. It was getting near to Christmas and her aunt and uncle drove her back to her home for her week's visit. Her aunt had written to Sofia's mother to tell her the good news and they were all greeted warmly. Her mother wondered if Sofia might be sent back home now that her sister was going to have her own baby but her aunt insisted that the arrangement should continue. They had grown fond of

Sofia and she was doing so well at school that it seemed a shame to disrupt things now.

Sofia was happy to see her family and her sisters, after an initial shyness, soon welcomed her back and they all settled into their old ways except that it was Christmas time so everything was that bit more joyous and exciting. Her aunt and uncle had left presents for the girls and also given them some food for the festive season so her mother was able to cook two chickens for Christmas Day and make some cakes and other treats.

The week after Christmas her uncle came to collect her to take her back to Athens. Sofia was happy to go back as she'd found their little cottage cramped and uncomfortable after the luxuries of the house in Athens. Her aunt was now being careful not to overdo things and she would go for a rest each afternoon and Sofia was instructed to be quiet and considerate and not make too much noise or disturb her aunt. She didn't find this difficult as she would read her books or do some colouring and each week she would write to her family.

In the late spring her aunt gave birth to a little girl. They called her Cinzia. Things were now different in the house in Athens. Sofia was no longer the focus of attention. Now it was all about Cinzia. Sofia didn't mind this. She was happy for her aunt and uncle and she was used to looking after her two younger sisters so was happy to help her aunt in as many ways as she could. She would change Cinzia's nappies and rock her to sleep in her arms to give her aunt a break. She went on errands for her aunt and played with Cinzia, making her laugh and keeping her amused. The time went quickly as Sofia worked hard at school and also worked hard at home.

She still visited her mountain home three times a year but her older two sisters seemed more grown up and distant now. They resented her taking up space in their bed at night and she felt obliged to cling to the edge of the bed and try not to take up too much room. Her two younger sisters were always pleased to see her because she brought them clothes she'd outgrown and other presents of books she'd read and toys she no longer played with. Her parents made good use of her when she was home as they encouraged her to teach her younger sisters things she'd been learning and to help them with their maths and other school subjects. Sofia was particularly good at maths and also helped her father with his bills and managing the farm. She helped her mother round the house and learned how to cook by watching her mother.

After the long summer break when she went back to Athens little Cinzia greeted her happily and she started a new year at school. She continued to work hard and strived to be the best in every subject and often succeeded. She loved Cinzia as much, if not more, than her sisters and they became very close. The years passed by and Sofia was now in the senior school and doing well. She decided to do mathematics at university and passed all her final exams with flying colours. She went to the university in Athens but still continued to live with her aunt and uncle. She worked just as hard at university and graduated with a first class honours degree. Her parents came to her graduation ceremony along with her aunt and uncle and everyone was happy for her. During her time at university she had often attended classes with a young man, Ioannis, who was doing the same course. They were rivals in class and vied with each other to be the top of the class. They graduated at the same time and she introduced him to her parents and aunt and uncle and she met his parents.

Once they both graduated they decided they didn't want to part so became engaged. She went to teach mathematics at a local school and he was articled into an accountancy firm in the city. Once he had qualified they married. Sofia bought five matching dresses for her sisters and Cinzia to be her bridesmaids and they had a big Greek wedding in Athens. Her aunt and uncle gave them a generous wedding present, as did his parents, so they were able to start their married life in a little flat in the centre of Athens.

For a couple of years they lived busy lives, both working hard until Ioannis was offered a position at a large firm in London. They relocated to London and Sofia was able to find a job teaching at a prestigious girls' school so she and Ioannis worked near each other. They were also able to put a deposit down on a house where they lived for the next ten years. During this time Sofia had three sons. She took time off work but soon went back to her job, employing au pair girls to look after her sons. She still had time with them during the holidays and would sometimes send money over to one of her younger sisters to come and stay with them for a holiday. Cinzia was always welcome and while she was still at school she would come over for holidays and help to look after the boys while also exploring London. Her parents declined offers to come and visit as they spoke no English and didn't think they would like the English weather but Sofia and Ioannis would take the boys back to Greece for holidays so that their parents could have a chance to get to know their grandsons.

Life was busy and fulfilling and the years passed by only too quickly. Sofia enjoyed her life in London, she relished being a mother and she loved working in the school and helping other girls to achieve their potential in the way that she had been helped. Each night when she went to bed she thought how lucky she had been to have been given so many opportunities. Yet, when she went to bed she would open the bedroom window, curl up in bed, close her eyes and often fancy she caught the scent of mountain flowers or could feel the breeze of fresh mountain air.